W9-BXP-611

Dedicated to Nelle Reneau— T.R.

Rabbit Ears Books is an imprint of Rabbit Ears Productions.
Published by Picture Book Studio Ltd., Saxonville, Massachusetts.

Printed in Hong Kong.
10 9 8 7 6 5 4

Library of Congress Cataloging in Publication Data
Kipling, Rudyard, 1865-1936.
How the camel got his hump / Rudyard Kipling; illustrated by Tim Raglin.
Summary: When the world was new, the camel, a creature of 'scruciating idleness, said "Humph!" too often and received for all time a hump[h] from Djinn of All Deserts.
ISBN 0-88708-096-0
ISBN 0-88708-097-9 (bk & cassette pkg)
[1. Camels–Fiction.] I. Raglin, Tim, ill. II. Title.
PZ7.K632Hf 1989
[E]–dc19 88-33366

written by Rudyard Kipling

HOW THE CAMEL GOT HIS HUMP

illustrated by Tim Raglin

Rabbit Ears Books

Now this is the next tale, and it tells how the Camel got his big hump.

In the beginning of years, when the world was so new and all, and the Animals were just beginning to work for Man, there was a Camel, and he lived in the middle of a Howling Desert because he did not want to work; and besides, he was a Howler himself. So he ate sticks and thorns and tamarisks and milkweed and prickles, most 'scruciating idle; and when anybody spoke to him he said *"Humph!"* Just *"Humph!"* and no more.

Presently the Horse came to him on Monday morning, with a saddle on his back and a bit in his mouth, and said, "Camel, O Camel, come out and trot like the rest of us."

"*Humph!*" said the Camel; and the Horse went away and told the Man.

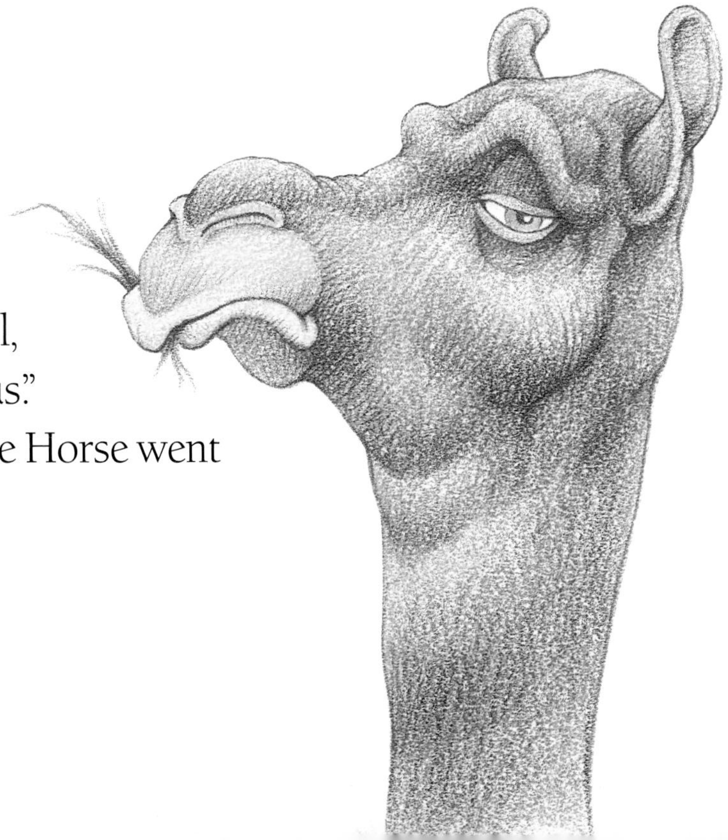

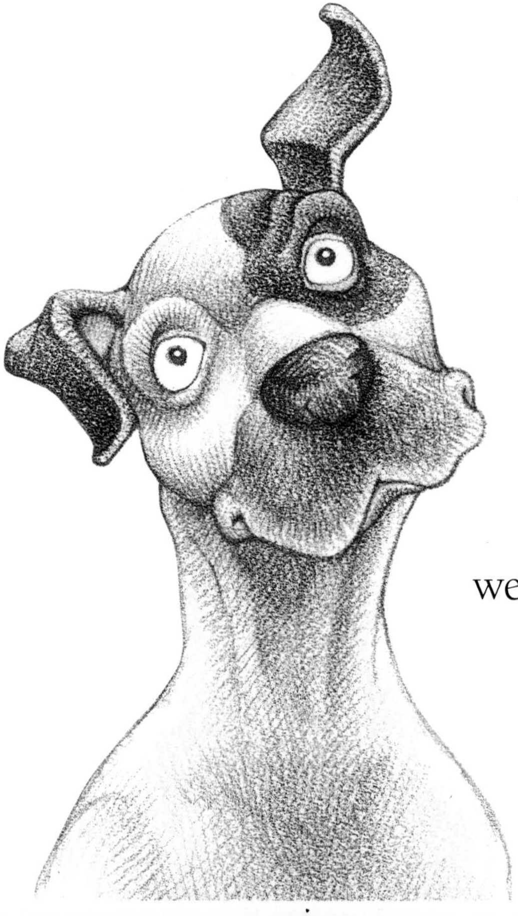

Presently the Dog came to him, with a stick in his mouth, and said, "Camel, O Camel, come and fetch and carry like the rest of us."

"Humph!" said the Camel; and the Dog went away and told the Man.

Presently the Ox came to him, with the yoke on his neck and said, "Camel, O Camel, come and plough like the rest of us."

"*Humph!*" said the Camel; and the Ox went away and told the Man.

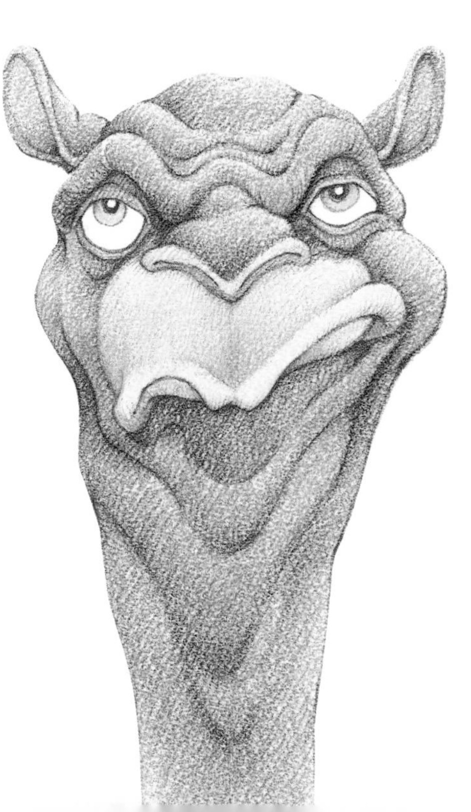

At the end of the day the Man called the Horse and the Dog and the Ox together, and said, "Three, O Three, I'm very sorry for you (with the world so new-and-all); but that Humph-thing in the Desert can't work, or he would have been here by now, so I am going to leave him alone, and you must work double-time to make up for it."

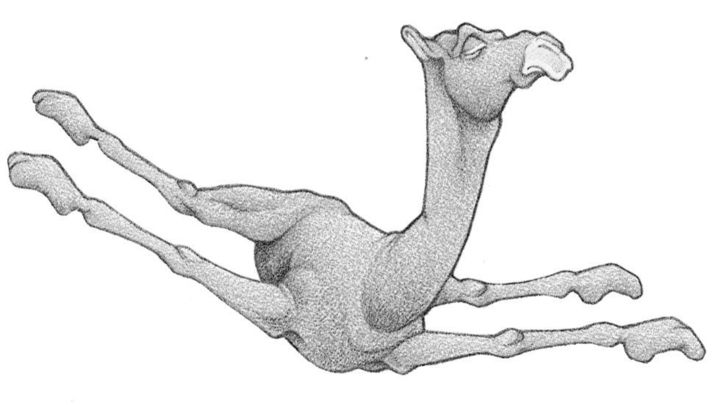

That made the Three very angry (with the world so new-and-all), and they held a palaver, and an *indaba*, and a *punchayet*, and a pow-wow on the edge of the Desert; and the Camel came chewing milkweed *most* 'scruciating idle, and laughed at them. Then he said *"Humph!"* and went away again.

Presently there came along the Djinn in charge of All Deserts, rolling in a cloud of dust (Djinns always travel that way because it is Magic), and he stopped to palaver and pow-wow with the Three.

"Djinn of All Deserts," said the Horse, "*is* it right for any one to be idle, with the world so new-and-all?"

"Certainly not," said the Djinn.

"Well," said the Horse, "there's a thing in the middle of your Howling Desert (and he's a Howler himself) with a long neck and long legs, and he hasn't done a stroke of work since Monday morning. He won't trot."

"Whew!" said the Djinn, whistling, "that's my Camel, for all the gold in Arabia! What does he say about it?"

"He says *'Humph!'* " said the Dog; "and he won't fetch and carry."

"Does he say anything else?"

"Only *'Humph!'*; and he won't plough," said the Ox.

"Very good," said the Djinn. "I'll humph him if you will kindly wait a minute."

The Djinn rolled himself up in his dust-cloak, and took a bearing across the desert, and found the Camel most 'scruciatingly idle, looking at his own reflection in a pool of water.

"My long and bubbling friend," said the Djinn, "what's this I hear of your doing no work, with the world so new-and-all?"

"*Humph!*" said the Camel.

The Djinn sat down, with his chin in his hand, and began to think a Great Magic, while the Camel looked at his own reflection in the pool of water.

"You've given the Three extra work ever since Monday morning, all on account of your 'scruciating idleness," said the Djinn; and he went on thinking Magics, with his chin in his hand.

"Humph!" said the Camel.

"I shouldn't say that again if I were you," said the Djinn; "you might say it once too often. Bubbles, I want you to work."

And the Camel said *"Humph!"* again, but no sooner had he said it than he saw his back, that he was so proud of, puffing up and puffing up into a great big lolloping humph.

"Do you see that?" said the Djinn. "That's your very own humph that you've brought upon your very own self by not working. To-day is Thursday, and you've done no work since Monday, when the work began. Now you are going to work."

"How can I," said the Camel, "with this humph on my back?"

"That's made a-purpose," said the Djinn, "all because you missed those three days. You will be able to work now for three days without eating, because you can live on your humph; and don't you ever say I never did anything for you. Come out of the Desert and go to the Three, and behave. Humph yourself!"

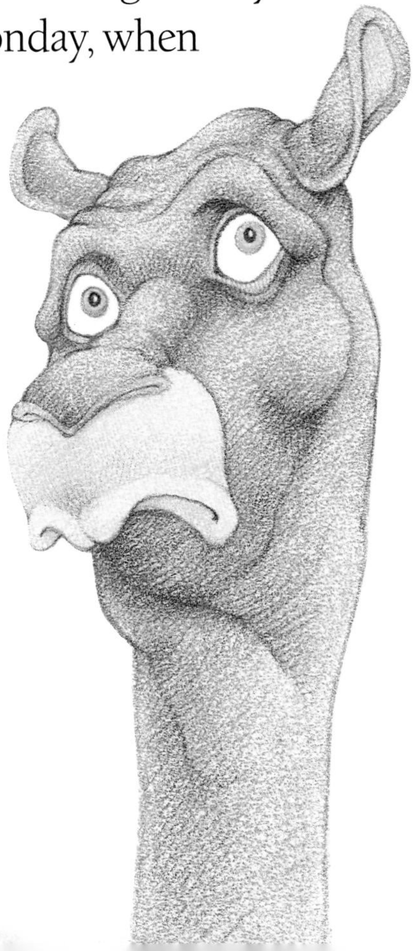

And the Camel humphed himself, humph and all, and went away to join the Three. And from that day to this the Camel always wears a humph (we call it "hump" now, not to hurt his feelings); but he has never yet caught up with the three days that he missed at the beginning of the world, and he has never yet learned how to behave.